EAST SCHOOL MEDIA CENTER
Torrington, CT 06790

D1116144

Discard

By the Same Author

Pishtosh, Bullwash & Wimple
Stewed Goose
The Great Green Turkey Creek Monster

(Margaret K. McElderry Books)

GRANDPA'S GHOST STORIES

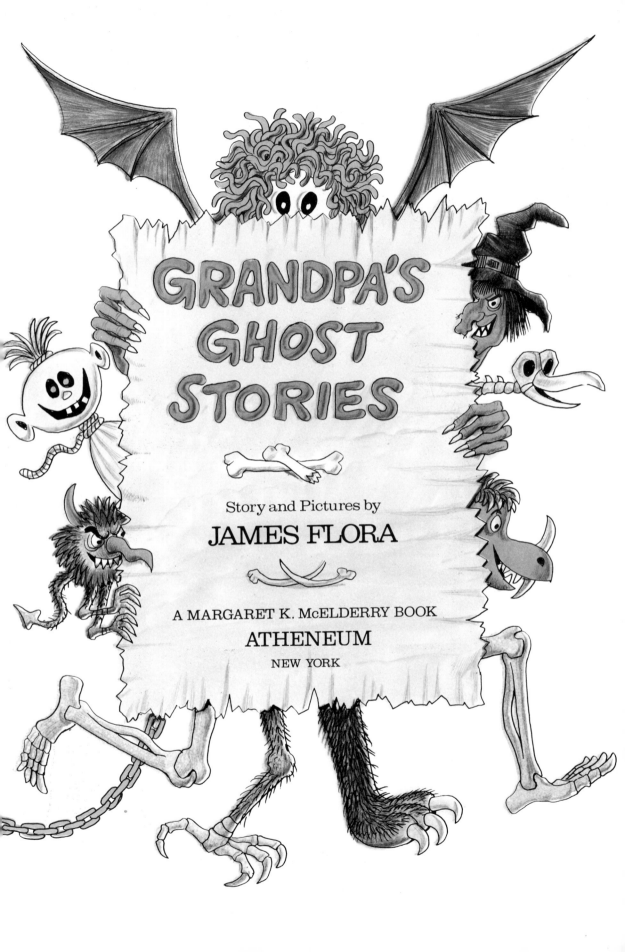

GRANDPA'S GHOST STORIES

Story and Pictures by

JAMES FLORA

A MARGARET K. McELDERRY BOOK

ATHENEUM

NEW YORK

This book is for
ANTHONY & PETER VIETRO
my favorite rollickers

Copyright © 1978 by James Flora
All rights reserved. No part of this book may
be reproduced or transmitted in any form or by
any means, electronic or mechanical, including
photocopying, recording, or by any information
storage and retrieval system, without permission
in writing from the Publisher.
Atheneum
Macmillan Publishing Company
866 Third Avenue, New York, NY 10022
Collier Macmillan Canada, Inc.
Printed in the United States of America
First Edition
7 9 11 13 15 17 19 20 18 16 14 12 10 8
Library of Congress catalog card number 78-51999
ISBN 0-689-50112-9

CRASH! GRUMBLE-RUMBLE!

Thunder cracked the sky and rain rattled the windows.
A wolf howled. A tree crashed to the ground.
It was a terrible stormy night outside.
Grandpa's house creaked and groaned.
KER-BLAM!
A bolt of lightning crashed on the roof.
I hopped onto Grandpa's lap.

"You're shaking like a cat in a room full of rocking chairs," Grandpa said. "Don't worry. There's a lightning rod on the roof. You're safe in here."

He filled his pipe and lit it.

"Just think how terrible it would be if you were lost in the woods in a storm like this. What would you do then?"

"I don't know, Grandpa. I think I'd just crawl under a log and die."

"No, you wouldn't," Grandpa said. "I know, because when I was your age it happened to me. I was lost in a forest but I didn't crawl under a log. I looked for a safe, dry place. I found one. An old woodcutter's shack deep in the forest.

"The door was open so I went inside, and that's where I found the bag of old bones. But that's a story too terrible to tell. It might scare the pants off you."

"Please, Grandpa. Please tell me the story," I begged.

"Very well. I don't mind if I do," Grandpa said.

The Bag of Old Bones

"There was nothing in that shack," Grandpa said. "Not a table. Not a chair. Not even a lamp or a candle. It was bare except for one thing — a big leather bag sat in one corner. It was covered with dust and tied at the neck with a thick leather thong.

"After I dried off a bit I took a look at the sack. I could see no marks on it. Just some cracks and bulges.

" *'Open me!'* said a hoarse voice.

"My hair stood on end. The voice came from inside the sack.

"But you know how boys are with sacks. They always want to know what's inside. So I opened it. I wish I hadn't. A fearful stench rose from the opening. I held my nose and looked inside.

"A grinning skull stared up at me.

" *'Thankee kindly, lad,'* said the skull in a cracked voice. *'I've been shut in this sack for nigh onto two hundred years and I'm dying for a breath of fresh air.'*

"The skull took a deep breath and coughed.

" *'Why don't you turn the sack upside down and help me put myself together?'*

"Well, I like puzzles, so I turned the sack over. Out spilled bones of all sizes and shapes. The skull cackled and sneezed.

" *'There's my neck bone and my shoulder bones. Just hook them together, if you please.'*

" *'Now the arm bones. Good. You are a smart little fellow. Now just fasten my hands to the arm bones. Fine. Great.'*

"The arm lifted with a creak and stretched its fingers.

"I found all of the little spine bones and fitted them together. It was a fine puzzle and I forgot what I was doing until the feet were fitted to the ankle bones.

"With a fearsome shriek the bones jumped up and pranced around the shack.

"It was horrible. I had never seen a skeleton before. Especially one that moved.

" '*As soon as I find my teeth we'll have a bit to eat,*' said the skeleton. '*It's been two hundred years since I've had a morsel in my mouth.*'

"He rooted around in the sack until he found his teeth. He popped them into his grinning jaws.

" '*Now we'll have dinner,*' he cackled. '*And the dinner is you. I'M-GOING-TO-EAT-YOU-UP!*'

"He grabbed me by the coat, but I slipped out of it. I ran from the shack so fast I tore the door off its hinges," Grandpa said. "I ran through the forest, bumping into trees and falling over rocks. Behind I could hear the clickety-clack of running bones.

"Just in time I saw a tiny cave in the hillside. I dove in and covered the door with a big rock. Whew! I was just in time. Outside I could hear the skeleton clawing at the rock.

"I thought I was lucky to be safe in that cave, but I wasn't. I was in worse trouble than ever. I had stumbled into the Cave of the Warty Witch. But that's another story, too terrible to tell."

"Please tell me, Grandpa," I begged. "I like terrible stories."

"Very well. I don't mind if I do," said Grandpa. "And I will if you will just turn the page."

The Cave of the WARTY WITCH

"It was so dark in the cave that I had to feel my face to see if it was still there. Suddenly a big fiery eye flicked open. Then another and another until at least a dozen evil yellow eyes were staring at me.

"Something hard and furry crawled up my leg. I screamed and jumped and stomped down on someone's foot.

" 'OUCH! YOU CLUMSY BEAST!' a cracked voice screeched. A bony hand slapped my face and scratched my cheek. Chills ran up my spine. Was it another skeleton?

"Suddenly the cave filled with light. There, nose to nose, staring into my eyes was a . . .

"WITCH!"

"She was a mean-looking, fearsome witch — with a witch's hat, witch's hair and a long sharp witch's nose covered with warts. And those eyes — witches eyes — brr-r-r. Like slits of fire.

"She limped around on her sore foot squealing at me.

" 'Did you see that, children. This beast broke into our happy home and almost broke my foot. What shall we do with him?'

"I looked around the cave, but I didn't see any children. It was filled with spiders. Huge, sticky, furry spiders with big, squishy mouths full of teeth. They squeaked and leaped about, nipping at my legs and ears.

" '*Be our brother. Be our brother*,' they squeaked.

" 'Hee-hee-hee,' cackled the witch. 'They want you to be a spider, like them. Once they were children until they broke into my home, just as you did. Now they are my spider family and, in a jiffy, you will be too.'

"She pulled a wishbone from her filthy clothes, struck my head with it and squealed,

'BONE OF WISHES, LISTEN TO ME,

MAKE THIS BOY A SPIDER

WHEN I COUNT THREE.'

" 'I don't want to be a spider,' I cried. I tried to run but the spiders threw me to the floor.

" 'ONE. TWO.'

"I closed my eyes and shivered.

" 'THREE!'

" '*SPLOK!*'

"In a flash I could feel myself changing. My body swelled up and my teeth grew long and sharp. My arms disappeared and hairy legs sprouted out all over me.

"The old witch led me to a mirror. I hardly dared to look. When I did, I saw a fearful, hairy spider. It was me. I looked exactly like my new brothers and sisters.

" 'Now spin me a nice strong web. I want to take a nap,' said the witch.

" 'But I don't know how,' I squeaked.

" 'Then you had better learn fast,' screeched the witch and she beat me with her broom.

"*Whack-whack-whack!*

"Oh it hurt. She almost broke my back. I tried to hide but the other spiders wouldn't let me. And before I knew it I was spinning a web. I don't know how I did it. I suppose it is something all spiders know without going to a web school.

"When the web was finished the witch climbed in and fell fast asleep. The spiders slept on the floor. So did I.

"I couldn't sleep though. I kept thinking about being a spider for the rest of my life. Crawling around this cold, dark cave, eating bugs and flies. It made me cry.

"Suddenly, through my tears, I saw the witch's arm hanging from her cobweb bed. The wishbone was in her hand.

"I grabbed it and said,

'BONE OF WISHES, LISTEN TO ME,

MAKE THIS SPIDER A BOY

WHEN I COUNT THREE.'

" 'ONE, TWO, THREE.'

"*SPLOK!*

"I was a boy again and I ran deep into the cave. Behind I could hear squeals and clicking claws as the spiders scuttled after me. The witch was screaming. Lights were flashing.

"In the nick of time I saw a hole at the end of the cave. I dove in.

"*It was too small!*

"My body stuck tight while my legs dangled in the cave. I shut my eyes waiting for a big spider mouth to bite them off.

"Then a hand grabbed my hair and pulled me out of the cave.

" 'Oh my! That was close,' I panted. 'You saved my life.'

"It was so dark and stormy that I couldn't see who had yanked me from the cave.

"Then, by the next flash of lightning, I saw that it was…

"*Nobody*.

"Just a big, cold, bony hand with no body. I got goose bumps.

"The hand squeezed me tight and soared off into the storm. I didn't care. I was so tired and wet and cold that I didn't care *what* was going to happen next."

"What did happen, Grandpa?"

"Worse things," he said. "Terrible things."

"Tell me about them, Grandpa. Please," I begged.

"Very well. I don't mind if I do," Grandpa said. "And I will if you will just turn the page."

The House of the GHASTLY GHOST

"That icy hand traveled fast. We zoomed over trees and dodged bolts of lightning until we came to a house deep in the forest.

"What a house! It was built of mud, blood, old bones and bat wings. Here and there you could see a shin bone or a withered claw sticking out of the walls. The roof was made of old rat fur and dead hair. Perched on top were the bones of a long-dead alligator. ·

"There were no doors or windows in this house. Right away I knew that it had to be the house of a ghost. Ghosts don't need doors or windows. They use the chimney.

"As we started down the chimney I heard a hollow voice wailing down below.

" *'Where is my hand? I want my sweet hand. Where are you, dear hand?'*

"As soon as we sailed out of the fireplace I saw her. What a fearsome sight! I got more goose bumps in between my goose bumps."

"She was huge! A monstrous white ghost. She floated just off the floor and her head nearly touched the ceiling. Her eyes and mouth were just gaping, black holes in her shroud. Her hair was ragged and squiggly.

"Beside her stood a giant werewolf, snarling and snaffling. His hair bristled like a bed of nails and his nasty yellow eyes searched me from head to toe. He showed me his long, sharp teeth and his fiery red tongue. I didn't like them.

"The ghost lifted an empty sleeve and whispered, '*Come, hand. I need you, darling. Come to me now.*'

"The hand floated to the sleeve and slipped into place. Then the ghost lifted me up to the horrible, black holes that were her eyes.

" '*You are a darling, boy. You shall be my very own sweet baby.*' She moaned and kissed me.

"UGH! Her breath smelled like the wind that blows from a cave full of bats. She hugged me close. WHOOF! Her shroud smelled even worse, like a toad's underwear.

"We floated across the room and she turned on her TV set.

" 'We'll have some fun until it's time for dinner.' She hummed and kissed me again.

"Have you ever seen ghost TV? It's on Channel 4½ and it is awful. I mean it is the worst ever.

"First we looked at *The Open Grave Show*. It began with a mess of moldy old ghouls popping out of their graves and stumbling over some cows. This made the ghouls angry. They all fetched axes and began to chop each other into pieces. This went on until there was only one ghoul standing on a pile of splintered bones and skulls. He was declared the winner and a lizard came out and pinned a medal on him.

"Next we looked at Mrs. Ghost's favorite program. It was about cooking and was called *Feeding Phantom Faces*. It opened with a big, fat-bellied demon in a tall white hat. He hauled in a big iron pot and showed us how to make soup out of a dead elephant. URK! Then an old blue witch taught us how to fry baby toes and eyeballs and bake a knuckle-bone pie.

"While all of this was going on, a screaming banshee orchestra was playing music that sounded like truck brakes.

"Then we saw a commercial for *Goblin Grease*. I didn't know that goblins needed grease but they do. It seems that their knees creak, and it is hard to sneak around houses with creaky knees. So they grease them up before they go spooking kids' houses.

"Last of all we looked at *The Hairy Snuffler Comedy Hour*, and I want to tell you that it was about as funny as a broken elbow. You know what hairy snufflers are, don't you? They're just big hairy blobs with lots of teeth and claws and runny noses.

"On this program a gang of snufflers went to school and ate up the whole second grade. One snuffler got all of the laughs by saying, over and over, 'Who's got the ketchup?'

"The show finished with another big laugh. The snufflers put whipped cream on the teacher and ate her for dessert.

"Mrs. Ghost and the werewolf laughed and giggled and roared. Mrs. Ghost laughed so hard that she dropped me.

"I never hit the floor. The werewolf gobbled me up in midair. As I was sliding down his throat I could hear Mrs. Ghost shouting at him.

" 'Oscar, that was naughty. You are such a greedy pig. You know very well that boys should be cooked before eaten. Their boots always make your stomach ache.'

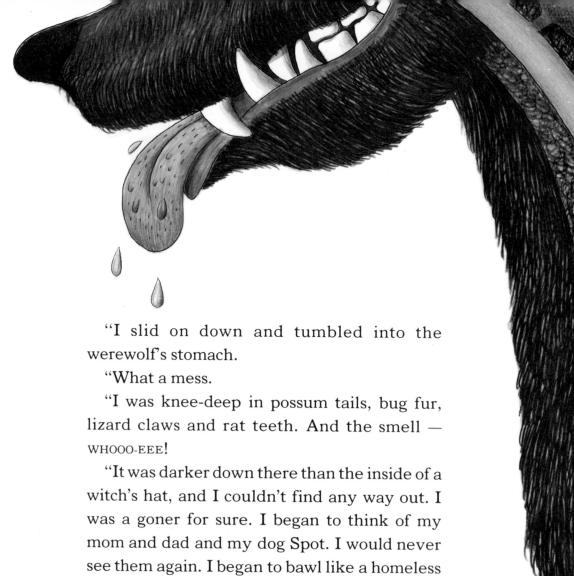

"I slid on down and tumbled into the werewolf's stomach.

"What a mess.

"I was knee-deep in possum tails, bug fur, lizard claws and rat teeth. And the smell — WHOOO-EEE!

"It was darker down there than the inside of a witch's hat, and I couldn't find any way out. I was a goner for sure. I began to think of my mom and dad and my dog Spot. I would never see them again. I began to bawl like a homeless baby.

"I reached for my handkerchief to dry my tears. What do you think I found in my pocket?

"*The witch's wishbone.*

"I prayed that it would work one more time.

'BONE OF WISHES, LISTEN TO ME,

AT THE COUNT OF THREE

I WANT TO BE

ROCKING AT HOME

WITH MY GRANDSON ON MY KNEE.

" '*ONE, TWO, THREE.*'

"*SPLOK!*

"The wishbone worked because here I am," Grandpa said.

"Aw, Grandpa. Is that story true? You just made it up, didn't you?"

"I don't think so," Grandpa said. "Because I still have this."

He fished in his pocket and pulled out the wishbone.

"Would you like to try it? What would you like to be? I'll wish it for you."

"Not tonight, Grandpa," I said. "It's too rainy out."

But I put the wishbone in my pocket and I've still got it.

One of these days when I get brave enough I'm going to try it out.

So if some dark night you find a goblin under your bed or a spook in the hall, come right up and shake its hand.

It will only be me.

And I never hurt a thing in my life...except a baseball.